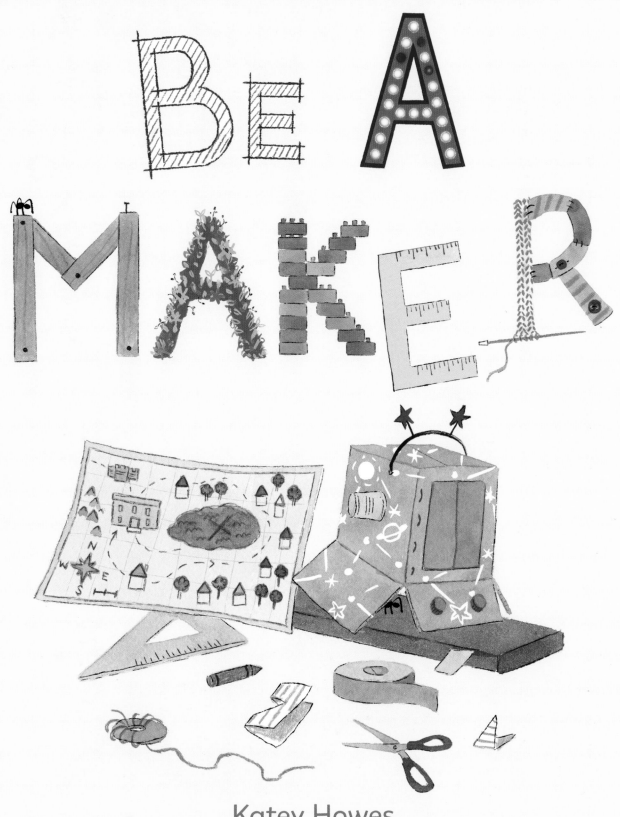

BE A MAKER

Katey Howes

illustrated by Elizabet Vuković

Carolrhoda Books · Minneapolis

For my mom and dad, who have always been proud of what I made —K.H.

For Nolletje & all makers, you are never too young or old to start making —E.V.

Carolrhoda Books
A division of Lerner Publishing Group, Inc.
241 First Avenue North
Minneapolis, MN 55401 USA

For reading levels and more information, look up this title at www.lernerbooks.com.

Designed by Emily Harris.
Main body text set in Mikado Medium 16/22.
Typeface provide HVD Fonts.
The illustrations in this book were created with watercolor, gouache, colored pencils, and Adobe Photoshop.

Library of Congress Cataloging-in-Publication Data

Names: Howes, Katey, author. | Vuković, Elizabet, illustrator.
Title: Be a maker / by Katey Howes ; illustrated by Elizabet Vuković.
Description: Minneapolis : Carolrhoda, [2019] | Summary: Illustrations and simple, rhyming text invite the reader to make everything from a tower to a charitable donation, alone or with neighbors.
Identifiers: LCCN 2018021908 (print) | LCCN 2018027771 (ebook) | ISBN 9781541541788 (eb pdf) | ISBN 9781512498028 (lb : alk. paper)
Subjects: | CYAC: Stories in rhyme. | Conduct of life—Fiction.
Classification: LCC PZ8.3.H8417 (ebook) | LCC PZ8.3.H8417 Be 2019 (print) | DDC [E]—dc23

LC record available at https://lccn.loc.gov/2018021908

Manufactured in the United States of America
1-43529-33327-7/27/2018

Ask yourself this question in the morning when you wake:
in a world of possibilities, today, what will you make?

Make a tower,
    make it tall.

Make it
balance,
wobble,
fall.

Make a mess,
or make, instead,

a universe inside your head.

Make a rhythm—drum and pound.

Ears make out another sound.

Make a telescope from toys.

See what's making all that noise.

Make a blueprint, make some more.

Cover desk

and wall

and floor.

Make your way to play outside.

Make a spaceship.

Take a ride.

Make a map to journey's end . . .

on the way, you make a friend.

Make a snack,
  and make a spare.

Make enough for both to share.

Make a plan,
and make a sign.

LEMONADE

50¢

Freshly
squee
zed

Have your neighbors make a line.

Make a gift of what you made.

Make a smile from lemonade.

Make a pledge to help some more.

Make a floor,
a wall,
a door.

Make a difference,
shine a light.

Make your town a team tonight.

Ask yourself this question as the sun begins to fade:

in a day of making choices,

are you proud of what you made?